For Ann Knowles—YP

For Katelyn Grace, and your cousins Ella
and Olivia (and Charlotte)—DM

Scholastic Australia
345 Pacific Highway Lindfield NSW 2070
An imprint of Scholastic Australia Pty Limited
PO Box 579 Gosford NSW 2250
ABN 11 000 614 577
www.scholastic.com.au

Part of the Scholastic Group
Sydney · Auckland · New York · Toronto · London · Mexico City
· New Delhi · Hong Kong · Buenos Aires · Puerto Rico

Published by Scholastic Australia in 2013.
Text and illustrations copyright © Scholastic Australia, 2013.
Text by Yvette Poshoglian.
Cover design, illustrations and inside illustrations by Danielle McDonald.

National Library of Australia Cataloguing-in-Publication entry

Author: Poshoglian, Yvette.
Title: Puppy trouble / Yvette Poshoglian; illustrated by Danielle McDonald.
ISBN: 9781742836577 (pbk.)
Series: Poshoglian, Yvette. Ella and Olivia; 5.
Target Audience: For primary school age.
Subjects: Dogs--Juvenile fiction
Pets--Juvenile fiction.
Other Authors/Contributors: McDonald, Danielle.
Dewey Number: A823.4

Typeset in Buccardi

Printed by McPherson's Printing Group, Maryborough, VIC.

Scholastic Australia's policy, in association with McPherson's Printing Group, is to use
papers that are renewable and made efficiently from wood grown in responsibly managed forests,
so as to minimise its environmental footprint.

10 9 8 7   15 16 17 / 1

By
Yvette Poshoglian

Illustrated by
Danielle McDonald

A Scholastic Australia Book

Chapter One

Ella and Olivia are sisters. Ella is seven years old. Olivia is five-and-a-half years old. Both girls go to big school together. Ella loves to play netball and Olivia loves to draw.

Ella and Olivia are jumping with excitement. For the last month, they have been counting down the days.

The calendar has lots of
large crosses on it.
'Only three days left, Olivia!'
says Ella.
'I can't wait!' Olivia puts an
'X' on the calendar.

Her handwriting is now very neat since she started school. On the weekend, the sisters are going to the pet shop to choose their puppy. They have wanted a dog FOREVER. Ella and Olivia will love their puppy and spoil him rotten! Maybe even more than they spoil Max. Their brother Max is only one-and-a-half years old. He has just learned to walk and is starting to talk.

Soon he won't stop talking.
Ella and Olivia also love
to talk. *Chatterboxes,* Mum
calls them.

'You have to look after
your puppy,' warns Dad.
'I'm going to
take him for
walks every
day,' Ella
promises.

'I'm going to scratch his tummy,' says Olivia. '**WOOF, WOOF**,' barks Max. Olivia leans over and gives Max a scratch on the tummy. The house is going to be very busy once the puppy arrives!

The girls work hard to get everything ready. Mum and Dad want them to look after the puppy properly, like big girls.

'The puppy will need lots of  water,' reminds Mum.

'Puppies also need lots of playtime,' Dad says. 'I've been saving this old tennis ball for you.' Dad hands Ella a stinky old tennis ball.

'Yuck!' says Ella. 'I'm going to buy our puppy a new ball!' She has been saving up her pocket money.

Finally, the calendar is full of crosses.
'No more days to cross off, Ella,' says Olivia. 'We're off to the pet shop!'
'Ready, girls?' Dad asks.
He has put towels down on the back seat of the car.

'Puppies can get very excited when they meet new people,' says Mum. 'That's why we have to put newspaper on the floor and towels in the car. Puppies are brand-new dogs. They still have to learn how to do everything. Puppies need to be toilet-trained.'

Ella and Olivia can't wait to get to the pet shop.

When they arrive, they rush to the window. There are all sorts of animals and people in there. There are babies looking at tropical fish.

There are grannies looking at pretty kittens.

There are big brothers looking at guinea pigs.

Olivia spots the puppies in the middle of the pet shop.
'The puppies are here!' cries Olivia. 'Come and look!'

Ella sees a little white mop with ears.
'That's a Maltese terrier,' Dad says.
Olivia spies a spotty dog.
'That's a Dalmatian,' Dad says.

Please take me home
I am a
Golden Retriever
I am 9 weeks old

But then Olivia and Ella
see the most perfect dog in
the world. He is sitting in
the corner all by himself.

He has yellow-white fur.
His blonde eyelashes are
very long. His black nose
is soft and wet. He looks
at Ella and Olivia with his
big, brown eyes.
'We have found our puppy!'
the girls cry.

Chapter Two

On the way home, the little puppy curls up on Olivia's lap. He shivers slightly. He is a bit scared. Right now, he is tiny enough to hold in two hands. But soon enough he is going to grow into a big, strong and very fluffy dog!
'There, there,' says Olivia.

'Don't be afraid. We are going to become best friends!' The puppy's fur is soft and shiny. His little eyelashes are so beautiful. Olivia has never seen anything so **PRECIOUS**.

Ella holds a new ball that she bought at the pet shop with her pocket money. It squeaks when squeezed. It is a present for the puppy.

SQUEAK!

SQUEAK!

SQUEAK!

'Ella!' cries Dad.
'I'm just practising, Dad,'
Ella says.

Together, they also bought
a dog brush, a leash, a
water bowl and some
special puppy food.

When they get home, they
let the puppy into the
backyard. The puppy is
not sure what to do. So he
sits on the grass. He looks
around. His little black
nose twitches in the air.

This is his new home.
Then **ZOOM!** He is off and
racing. He sniffs the roses.

He licks the fence. He
inspects the clothes line.

Mum falls in love with the
puppy straight away.

'He is adorable!' gushes Mum. 'I love golden retrievers.'

'They are smart and funny, and very loyal,' nods Dad.

'*Ruff!*' barks Max.

The puppy spends the afternoon exploring. He disappears into the shed. He crawls under the garden hose. He even tries to bark.

'*Woof!*' goes the puppy.

Then he sees a bird in a tree.

WOOF! WOOF! WOOF!

'What are we going to call him?' Olivia asks.

'Well, he is a *Golden Retriever*. What about *GReg*?' says Mum.

'What about *GRaham*?' suggests Dad.

'You can't call a dog Graham!' says Mum.

But Ella has an idea.

'I think we should call him Bob,' says Ella. Everyone looks at the puppy.

24

'Bob!' Ella calls softly. The puppy stops mid-sniff. He turns to look at Ella.

'BOB!' Ella cries. Then she rushes over to give him a big hug.

'I think we have a dog called Bob,' laughs Dad.

The girls need to feed Bob.
Puppies eat **A LOT**! They
also poop a lot. Ella taps
on the can with her spoon.
Bob ignores her. But as
soon as she puts the food in
his bowl, he trots over, nose
twitching.

Everything he does is so
cute. Olivia fills up his
water bowl. Together, they
watch him eat and drink.

'I'm very proud of you, girls,' says Dad. 'But don't forget to clear out everything in the laundry. That is where Bob is going to sleep.'

'Looking after a puppy is a lot of hard work,' Mum reminds them. Ella and Olivia look at each other. They think having a puppy is really easy!

Chapter Three

When it is time to go to bed, Ella and Olivia give Bob special cuddles. Already, he is a very SPOILED puppy.

'Good night, Bob,' Ella whispers.

'Sweet dreams, Bob,' Olivia says softly.

Bob looks at them with his big, brown eyes. They take him to the laundry, where he will sleep tonight.

Ella and Olivia cover the floor with pieces of old newspaper, just in case Bob has an accident.

Bob has his own little dog bed to sleep on. It is just his size. Bob sniffs around the laundry until he finds his bed. He puts one paw on the bed, then another. Then he jumps up and finds a comfortable spot.

Soon, Bob is snoring little puppy snores. His little blonde eyelashes don't even flutter. It has been a big day with his new family. He is a tired puppy.

In the morning, the girls leap out of bed. They can't wait to see Bob!

But when Ella opens the laundry door, she gets a big shock. The laundry is such a mess. The clothes have been pulled out of the laundry basket and thrown around the room. A pair of ugg boots has been ripped to pieces. Bob's new bed has fluff spilling out of it.

Water from his bowl is sloshed across the floor. And Bob's paw prints are everywhere! Bob sits in the middle of the mess, waggling his tail.

'*Woof!*' he says. He looks very pleased with himself. 'Uh-oh,' Ella says. Bob has been very naughty! But he's only little and he hasn't been taught not to rip things up yet.

'What happened here, Bob?' Olivia asks. Then she can't resist giving him another special cuddle. So does Ella.

Mum and Dad are not amused. The laundry is a complete mess!

'Not my ugg boots, Bob!' Dad moans, holding up a half-chewed boot. 'That was my favourite pair!'

Ella and Olivia go red.
They did not get things
ready before Bob went
to bed. Ella and Olivia were
supposed to put everything
away. They *completely forgot*.

'Do you know what this means, girls?' Mum says in her serious voice. 'Bob is your puppy. He is your responsibility. You have to clean up after him.'

Ella and Olivia groan.
'But I want to play with Bob,' says Ella.
'Me too,' says Olivia.

'You can play with Bob once you have cleaned up

his mess,' Dad says. 'That's part of the job of having a new puppy.'

Ella and Olivia grumble. Bob has been quite disgusting. They pick up the clothes and put them in the washing machine. Ella gets a mop and cleans up Bob's paw prints. Olivia picks up the fluff from the ugg boots and throws it in the bin.

38

'Bob, you are a messy boy!'
Olivia says. Bob looks at
them with his brown eyes.
'Awwww, Bob, we can't be
stern with you for long,'
Ella laughs.

'Let's go and play, boy!'
cry Ella and Olivia.

Chapter Four

Ella and Olivia try to teach Bob to go fetch, but he's not very good at it. When they throw the ball, he runs after it, but he doesn't give it back. Bob hangs onto the ball and runs around with it in his mouth. It just fits.

Ella, Olivia and Dad take Bob for his first walk. Bob

doesn't want to wear a leash. But he does want to stop and sniff everything on the street.

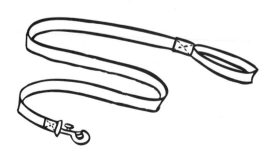

'Hold onto the leash tightly,' Dad says. 'That way he will learn what to do.' Bob is pulling left and right. He doesn't want to walk in a straight line.

'Bob wants to stop and smell the roses,' says Dad. 'This way, Bob,' says Olivia helpfully.

Ella is having a hard time getting Bob to walk down the footpath.

He keeps tugging her in all sorts of directions!

He is only a little puppy, but he is very strong.

'Be a good boy, Bob!' she cries.

Bob stops to sniff under
Mr Macpherson's gate.
Mr Macpherson is their
neighbour. He doesn't like
animals much. Or people.
Ella and Olivia are a bit
scared of him.

'There's nothing there,
Bob!' Ella stamps her foot.
She has had enough. Bob
has a lot to learn about
going for a walk.
'Here you go, Olivia.'

But just as Ella hands Olivia the leash, Bob sniffs hard. Then he **TAKES OFF!** The leash slips through both Olivia's and Ella's hands.

Oh no, Bob has escaped!

'BOB!' Ella cries.

'BOB! Come back!' shouts Dad.

'BOB! **BOB! BOB!**' Olivia yells.

But it is too late. Bob scampers swiftly over Mr Macpherson's lawn and runs under the sprinkler. Droplets of water cling to his fur as he runs up the front steps of the house. The front door is wide open. Bob shakes the water off his coat and disappears inside.

Ella and Olivia spring into action. Ella climbs over the gate and Olivia follows her. Dad shakes his head and pushes it open. *Ella and Olivia have a LOT to learn about dogs and gates,* thinks Dad.

Ella and Olivia race across the lawn and through the sprinkler. They shake themselves off at Mr Macpherson's front door, just like Bob.

'We're coming in, Mr Macpherson,' cries Ella. She is a bit scared. There is no reply. She steps through the door and into the dark hallway. There is no sign of Bob inside.

Olivia calls softly to Bob. 'Where are you, boy?'

Just when the girls are about to give up, they see Bob run out of a bedroom up ahead. His leash trails after him.

'There he is!' points Ella. 'We've got to get him!'

Together Ella and Olivia scramble down the hallway. Bob's leash is getting further away.

Suddenly, they find themselves standing in Mr Macpherson's kitchen. There are pots and pans hanging from the ceiling. They can smell toast and jam. Sitting at a small table is Mr Macpherson. He has grey hair, little wire spectacles and white, woolly eyebrows.

'Is this who you are looking for?' he smiles.

Chapter Five

Bob is sitting on Mr
Macpherson's lap,
nibbling on some toast
and jam. He looks very
comfortable, and so does
Mr Macpherson.

'*Woof!*' says Bob when he
sees the two girls.

'Phew!' say Ella and Olivia.
They are very happy to
see Bob!

'Sit down, girls,' Mr Macpherson waves them in. 'Have some toast.'

Mr Macpherson strokes Bob's fur. 'This dog here is a good boy,' he says. 'He jumped up onto my lap straight away.'

'Really?' Dad asks, arriving in the kitchen. He is surprised to see everyone eating toast. Including Bob.

'He ran away,' says Ella.
'Too quickly for us,'
adds Olivia.
Mr Macpherson looks
thoughtfully at Bob.
'How old did you say this
puppy is?' he asks.
'Nine weeks old,' says Ella.
'He is a golden retriever.'
'Golden retrievers are very
good dogs. But when they
are this young, you have
to train them,' says Mr
Macpherson.

'You have to be very firm with puppies. Otherwise they will never learn how to do things the right way.'

Olivia puts down her toast and picks up Bob's leash. Bob's training needs to start right away. 'Come on, Bob. Time to go home!'

Ella, Olivia and Dad wave
goodbye to Mr Macpherson.

Olivia is in charge of walking Bob home. 'Come on, Bob,' she says **FIRMLY**. 'Let's go home.' All the way home, Bob is a good boy. He sniffs only a few flowers. He chomps only a few beetles. Olivia holds onto the leash very tightly. Soon, Bob gets the hang of walking down the street. When they get back home, they take his leash off.

Bob is already off on his next big adventure. He rips through the house, and roars out into the garden. This time, he is safe in the backyard. He can't go missing there!

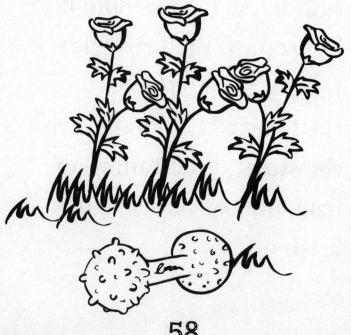

'We nearly lost Bob,' Ella says in a small voice. She is very glad they found him. 'Yes, I was worried sick!' Olivia blurts out.

It has been a big weekend, and Ella and Olivia have learned many new things. The two girls will get better at taking Bob for his walks and cleaning the laundry.

They also want to teach Bob good manners and new tricks. They are going to teach him how to play fetch, roll over and shake hands.

'Well done, girls!' smiles
Mum, hugging them both.
'I am very proud of you.
It's not easy looking after
a puppy.'

Ella and Olivia sigh loudly.
It is time to clean up again!
They hide all the shoes
in the house. They put all
their favourite books out
of reach. They learn how
to pick up Bob's poop in a
special plastic bag.

They put Bob's toys away
in a basket for next time.
Ella fills up his food bowl
with dry biscuits. Olivia
plumps up the cushion on
Bob's bed.

The girls are very tired,
and so is Bob after his big
adventure. He gives Ella
and Olivia a little lick, then
jumps up on his bed. Soon
he is fast asleep, dreaming
of ugg boots and toast
and jam.

ella AND Olivia

COLLECT THEM ALL!

Cupcake Catastrophe

Best Friend Showdown

Ballet Stars

The New Girl

Puppy Trouble

The Big Sleepover

Pony Problem

Cool Kitties

The Christmas Surprise

Sports Carnival

Flower Power

Christmas Wonderland

Beach Holiday

Friends Forever Stories

Super Sweet Stories

To find
out more go to:
EllaandOlivia.com.au
where you can play games
and do more
fun stuff!